THE TREASURE DRAGONS

DRAGON GIRLS

Aisha the Sapphire Treasure Dragon

Maddy Mara

DRAGON GIRLS

Aisha the Sapphire Treasure Dragon

by Maddy Mara

Scholastic Inc.

Text copyright © 2021 by Maddy Mara
Illustrations by Thais Damião, copyright © 2021 by Scholastic Inc

All rights reserved. Published by Scholastic Inc., *Publishers since 1920.* SCHOLASTIC and associated logos are trademarks and/or registered trademarks of Scholastic Inc.

The publisher does not have any control over and does not assume any responsibility for author or third-party websites or their content.

This book is a work of fiction. Names, characters, places, and incidents are either the product of the author's imagination or are used fictitiously, and any resemblance to actual persons, living or dead, business establishments, events, or locales is entirely coincidental.

ISBN 978-1-338-68067-6

10 9 8 7 6 5 4 3 2 1   21 22 23 24 25

Printed in the U.S.A. 40

First printing 2021

Book design by Stephanie Yang

Aisha and her grandmother pushed open the wooden door of the antique store. It creaked loudly. Aisha loved coming here. The store was filled with very old, very interesting things: rich tapestries, heavy chests, fancy vases, paintings with thick golden frames. There was even a suit of armor near the door. It was the kind of place where you might find something special in a dusty corner.

The days Aisha spent with her grandmother were the best. They always had lunch, and then visited the antique store. Looking at treasures from the past was their all-time favorite thing to do together.

"Let's look at the jewelry," Aisha's grandmother suggested.

The jewelry was displayed in a glass cabinet at the back of the store. Aisha and her grandmother loved trying on all the old pieces. Now that Aisha was doing a jewelry-making course, she liked looking at the old rings and necklaces to get ideas for her own creations.

"I'll be there in a moment," Aisha replied. "I'll just take a quick look around first."

Aisha had a quivery, excited feeling in her stomach. The moment she stepped inside the store today, she knew something was going to happen. Something magical. Recently, Aisha had been to a very special place with her friends Mei and Quinn called the Magic Forest. There, the three girls had discovered they were Treasure Dragon Girls! This meant that they could do all kinds of cool things like fly and roar powerful, magical roars. They were also good at finding treasure and protecting it. Aisha couldn't wait to go back.

Aisha looked down at the friendship bracelet on her wrist. She, Mei, and Quinn had made matching bracelets in jewelry class. Each had chosen a different color. Mei had picked ruby-red, and Quinn jade green. Aisha's favorite gemstone was sapphire, so in the center of Aisha's bracelet was a gorgeous blue bead. She picked blue whenever she could—for her clothes, her pencil case, even her hair ties.

As Aisha looked at the bracelet, something strange began to happen. Was she imagining it, or was the bead glowing like real sapphire?

Aisha rushed to the window so she could inspect the bead more clearly. Outside the antique store, snow covered the ground. The light was already starting to fade even though it was still afternoon. Aisha made a face. She hated winter. This was another reason why she longed to go back to the Magic Forest. It was so warm and bright there. She stared curiously at the bead in her bracelet again. It was definitely glowing.

Then Aisha heard someone singing. It wasn't

her grandmother or the shopkeeper. They were busy talking together. Aisha listened more carefully to the words:

Magic Forest, Magic Forest, come explore . . .

Aisha spun around. Hanging on a nearby wall was a large tapestry. She had always loved tapestries. From a distance they looked like paintings, but up close you could see every single perfect stitch. Aisha gazed at the scene in the tapestry. A snow-covered landscape of trees and mountains glistened like a diamond.

Aisha leaned in. The singing seemed to be

coming from the tapestry itself! Aisha felt her heart beating. Was she imagining it, or were the woven trees in the tapestry swaying, just a little? She took a step closer. She could almost smell the dark, smoky scent of pine cones in winter. Aisha was certain she could even hear the woven leaves on the tapestry trees rustling!

There was a sudden warmth on Aisha's wrist. The bead in her friendship bracelet was glowing even more brightly now. A sudden blue beam of light shot out from it, lighting up the tapestry, as though the sun had broken through the clouds. A snowy white path seemed to open up between the trees. Aisha could hear birdsong. The singing was getting louder and closer:

Magic Forest, Magic Forest, come explore...

The moment Aisha heard the words, she knew what was going on. It was time to visit the Magic Forest again! Aisha glanced over at her grandmother. She was still deep in conversation with the shop owner. Luckily, her grandmother could talk forever! With a thumping heart, Aisha turned back to the tapestry. She reached out to touch it, expecting to feel the ancient cloth beneath her fingers. But instead, her hand passed straight through the tapestry... and touched the rough bark of a tree trunk! A little creature darted through the undergrowth. The blue of Aisha's bracelet glowed ever brighter.

Stepping into a tapestry seemed like an impossible idea. But then again, being a Dragon Girl also seemed impossible. And yet that was definitely true! Taking a deep breath, Aisha chanted the words that were swirling around in her head:

Magic Forest, Magic Forest, come explore.
Magic Forest, Magic Forest, hear my roar!

Aisha stepped forward. With a whooshing

sound and a gust of cold air, the dusty antique shop faded away. Instead of being surrounded by old vases and brass lamps, Aisha was surrounded by tall trees. Yes! She was back in the Magic Forest!

2

Aisha was so excited to be back in the forest that it took her a moment to notice that something strange was going on. The last time she had been here, it had been warm and summery. But now the air was frosty, and thick snow blanketed the ground, just like at home. Maybe she wasn't in the Magic Forest after all?

As she looked down, Aisha caught sight of her reflection in a frozen puddle at her feet. Normally when she looked in the mirror, Aisha saw a girl with short dark hair, deep brown eyes, and a friendly smile. But now instead she saw something very different!

She looked down to see the strong, blue-scaled dragon body that was her incredible form in this magical place. *I must be in the Magic Forest after all*, thought Aisha. She turned her long neck to admire the huge and powerful wings on her back. They were sapphire blue, like the rest of her, and were decorated with silver and gold. Aisha thought her wings were the very best thing about being a Dragon Girl. And just because it was so fun, Aisha gave a loud roar. Bright blue flames flared from her mouth. Aisha ginned in satisfaction. There was no doubt her roar was working!

"But why it is so cold and snowy?" Aisha wondered out loud.

"You're here! You're here!" cried an excited voice from nearby.

Aisha turned to see a fluffy puppy leaping joyfully through the snow. He had gold markings around his face and his fur was a rich, dark blue. But that wasn't the strangest thing about this happy, talking canine. He also had wings! The puppy skidded to a stop at Aisha's feet, flipped over, and fell with a gleeful splat into the snow.

"Here, little guy. Let me help you up." Aisha laughed. She gently lifted the tiny creature from the snow and set him down on his paws.

"Thanks!" he said, shaking himself and sending snow flying. "I'm PlushyPup. I'm here to take you to the Tree Queen. We must hurry! The Shadow Sprites are getting stronger and stronger."

A thought struck Aisha. "Is that why it's snowing?" she asked.

PlushyPup nodded. "In the Magic Forest, it normally only snows high in the mountains, where I live with my family. But ever since the Shadow Sprites stole the treasure from the forest's vaults, the snow has been spreading. Now it's almost everywhere!"

"Why would the Shadow Sprites want to make the forest all snowy?" Aisha asked.

"The Shadow Queen and her sprites are most powerful in winter. And winter is when the forest is at its weakest. Also, it's easier for the Shadow Sprites to sneak around," explained

PlushyPup. "They love the cold and can move really quickly over snow."

Aisha shivered. *If the snow is everywhere, then the Shadow Sprites are everywhere, too.*

Aisha had noticed that when the sprites were nearby, she felt unsure of herself. That was how she felt right now. Nervously, Aisha glanced around. All she could see were the long shadows of the trees. But as she watched, the shadows started growing. They slipped across the ground toward her and PlushyPup.

"Quick, let's go!" Aisha called.

She gave her broad and powerful wings a mighty flap and rose into the air. PlushyPup shot up beside her, his stumpy little wings fluttering so fast they were just blue blurs.

The Shadow Sprites leapt at Aisha and PlushyPup.

"You won't get away!" they whispered. "You may as well give up now."

But there was no way Aisha was going to give up. She hadn't even gotten started! She kicked away the grasping sprites with her strong legs.

"Leave us alone," she roared fiercely.

Her roar glowed blue in the air, creating a bubble of warmth around her and PlushyPup. Aisha felt very determined. *Those sprites will not beat us*, she promised herself.

Aisha rose higher into the air. "Come on, PlushyPup," she called to the little puppy. "Let's get to the Tree Queen."

Immediately, PlushyPup zoomed ahead. "This way!" he barked.

As they sped away from the Shadow Sprites, Aisha looked down at the Magic Forest laid out below her. The landscape was so different from the last time she'd been here. Winter had taken hold of the entire forest. Aisha could see that the rivers had frozen over. Icicles hung like candle wax from tree branches. It was beautiful but strange. The Magic Forest wasn't meant to be like this!

It wasn't just how the forest looked, either. The last time Aisha had been here, the air had been heavy with the scent of tropical fruit, like mango, pineapple, and coconut. Now it smelled blank and cold. The worst part was that Aisha could see shadowy shapes slithering across the snow down below.

We've got work to do, thought Aisha. *But with Mei and Quinn's help, we will fix this!*

"We're almost there," called PlushyPup in his gruff little voice.

Sure enough, up ahead Aisha spotted the glade where the Tree Queen lived. This was the glowing heart of the Magic Forest. Protected by a force field, the glade shimmered like a magical snow globe. Even from up here, Aisha could see a tall and elegant tree at its center. Her leaves sparkled and shone in the sunlight.

Aisha felt a smile creep across her face. She could not WAIT to get this adventure started.

Aisha landed gently in the snow beside the force field.

PlushyPup hovered by her face, pushing his fuzzy snout against her cheek. "I can't go in the glade," he explained, "but I'll see you again soon."

With his fluffy tail wagging at full speed, the puppy flew off. Aisha was sad to see him

go, but she was
thrilled to be going
into the glade. It
looked so lovely and
warm in there, for
one thing!

She pushed one
paw through the force field. Instantly, warmth
covered it like a glove. She pulled her paw out
again and it was wrapped in cold once more.
The glade formed an unchanging bubble of
perfect spring weather. Aisha poked her head
through the dancing air of the force field. It
was strange to have her face so warm while
the rest of her was so cold.

Two dragons already hovered in the glade, just above the lush grass, watching Aisha closely. One dragon was the bright color of rubies, and the other was a rich jade green.

Mei, the ruby dragon, and Quinn, the jade dragon, were Aisha's friends from jewelry class. You could tell they were Treasure Dragons because they had silver and gold on their wings, like Aisha.

"Is the rest of you coming in, too?" Mei asked, looking like she was trying very hard not to laugh. "We have a quest to go on, you know."

"Oops! Sorry," said Aisha, stepping completely into the glade and warming up her whole body.

As she did, the majestic tree in the center

began to sway. The wooden branches softened into long arms, the leaves of the tree turned into flowing hair, and a kind, ageless face appeared. Within moments, the tall tree had transformed into the Tree Queen! Her warm brown eyes greeted each of them in turn.

"Welcome back, Treasure Dragons! I'm relieved you're here. As I am sure you've noticed, the Magic Forest is not as it should be. A strange winter has arrived. The snow is spreading far and wide."

"I've heard that the Shadow Sprites are stronger in winter," said Aisha.

"It's true," agreed the Tree Queen. "But that's

not all. The snow
makes it easier
for the sprites to
hide the objects
they have stolen
from the forest's
vault. As you know, the longer the treasure is
out of the vault, the more problems it causes
for the forest. You three have already found
the Forest Book, thank goodness. But now you
must find the Magic Mirror. If it isn't returned
to the vault soon, the Magic Forest may be
wintry forever."

The Treasure Dragons looked at one

another in dismay. Snow could be fun, but the Magic Forest was supposed to be warm and springlike!

Aisha shivered even though the air in the glade was warm. "We'll find that Magic Mirror," she vowed. "Come on, let's head off right now!"

"I love your enthusiasm, Aisha." The Tree Queen smiled. "But first there are some things you need to know." The queen's wavy hair billowed in the glade's gentle breeze. "As the name suggests, this is no normal mirror. You will know when you've found it. It feels ... different."

"Like the Forest Book was no normal book," said Mei.

The Tree Queen nodded. In their last quest,

the Treasure Dragons had recovered the Forest Book, an ancient and magical text that held all the secrets of the forest.

"You must be on your guard at all times," continued the Tree Queen, "for the Magic Mirror is very powerful."

"What does it actually do?" Quinn asked softly. She was the shy one of the group.

"Good question. If you look into the mirror, you will see yourself. But you won't see how you really look. Instead, you will see all the things you worry about. If you sometimes think you have a funny nose, you will have a VERY funny nose. If you worry about not feeling brave, fear will show on your face," explained the Tree

Queen. "This is why the Magic Mirror belongs in the vault. There it is safe, and use- ful. It reflects all the things that are starting to go

wrong in the forest and shows us what will happen if we don't step in and fix them. This means we can keep an eye on whether the glow bees have enough glow honey, for instance, or if the Rainberries are growing properly. Even if the golden sunflowers are not bright enough, the mirror can warn us about it. So you can see that the Magic Mirror is a very important tool. But it is dangerous when animals—even dragons!—look into it."

"So it's kind of like a magnifying glass for your worries?" Aisha asked.

"Exactly," the Tree Queen said. "To make it worse, things go very wrong in the forest when the mirror is not in the vault. That's why there is suddenly so much snow. The forest is out of balance."

It was a lot to take in. This was a very important quest!

"Aisha, you're in charge this time, so these

are for you," said the Tree Queen. She held out the compass and the bag that the Treasure Dragons had used during their last quest.

Aisha slipped on the bag. It fit neatly against her body. When Mei had worn the bag on their last quest, it had been covered with glittering rubies. Now that Aisha was wearing it, the rubies had transformed into beautiful sapphires to match her scales.

She put the compass over her neck like a long necklace. "I know we can only ask the compass one question, but it's good to have such a powerful tool to help us."

"The compass is powerful," agreed the Tree Queen. "But the most powerful thing you have is the bond between you three. The Shadow Sprites will try to divide you. It's important that you watch out for one another. Stick together, no matter what."

Aisha looked at Mei and Quinn. The three friends smiled.

"We will!" Aisha promised.

Going to jewelry class with Mei and Quinn
was the best. But since discovering she was
a Dragon Girl, Aisha had to admit that flying
with her friends was even better! She loved the
way her huge blue, silver, and gold wings cruised
the air currents. Using her wings had taken a
bit of getting used to, but now she felt strong

and sure when she flew high above the forest. She would never grow tired of feeling the breeze on her face and the drop in her stomach when she swooped low and then surged higher into the sky. Flying was better than any roller coaster in the world! And she loved being up so high that the forest stretched out like a lush carpet down below.

But today the forest didn't look like a lush carpet at all. The forest colors were all gone. Everything was covered in thick white snow. There were no birds hopping from branch to branch, no butterflies flitting around bright flowers.

The only movement Aisha could see were

gray shadows gliding silently across the snow. She frowned. She wasn't crazy about snow, and she definitely didn't like Shadow Sprites!

So let's get that Magic Mirror back into the vault, as fast as we can! Aisha told herself.

She looked across at Mei and Quinn and saw

that the determination on her friends' faces matched hers.

As they flew over a clearing, Aisha saw a huge pink fluffy ... *thing*. What was it? The object looked like a cloud at sunset, except the sun wasn't setting, and the cloudlike thing was on the ground. Mei and Quinn had spotted the pink thing, too.

"Is it a swarm of Shadow Sprites in disguise?" Quinn suggested.

Mei looked doubtful. "I don't think so. It's too puffy. It looks more like a giant blob of cotton candy. Should we check it out?"

"Okay," said Aisha. "But let's get ready to roar if it turns out to be a pack of Shadow Sprites."

In a triangle formation, the Treasure Dragons flew lower and lower. As they landed softly on the snow, Aisha saw that the pink cloud thing was actually a herd of pink sheep, all pressed together. Up close, their fleeces looked more like spun sugar than ever. They even smelled sweet!

The pink sheep were all pushing and shoving at one another, bleating mournfully. "I've always wanted lovely fleece. But mine is just all wrong!"

"Mine is far too thick and woolly. I want to shave it all off right now," baaed another sheep.

"What about me? I can't believe how pink I am. It clashes horribly with my eyes. I wonder if I should dye my fleece?"

"At least you can fix your problems," cried another sheep. "I can't seem to remember anything. Do you know what we're all even doing here?"

"What's going on?" whispered Quinn.

"I'll see if I can find out," said Aisha.

She flew into the air and hovered over the

fluffy pink sheep. The sheep were so distracted, they didn't even notice a Dragon Girl hovering above them. It was hard to see exactly, but there seemed to be something in the middle of the field. Whatever it was, the sheep kept jostling to get closer, bleating grumpily at one another. Aisha caught a quick glimpse of the thing—was that a frozen puddle?

But why would the sheep want to look into that? It didn't make sense.

Aisha flew so low that she was almost touching the fluffy pink sheep. Now she could see for sure—that wasn't a frozen puddle at all. It was something far more exciting! Quickly, she flew back to her friends. "I think they've got the Magic Mirror!" she told Mei and Quinn.

"How can you tell?" asked Mei.

"It has a beautiful gold frame," Aisha explained. "With the shapes of vines and flowers carved into it. But mostly it's because I can *feel* it's different. Just like the Tree Queen said. And it's obviously affecting the sheep."

"If you're right," said Mei excitedly, "then this is going to be the easiest quest ever!"

"Hmm, maybe not," said Quinn, tilting her head. "The Tree Queen warned us that the mirror was very powerful."

"Good point," said Mei. "So how do we get it back?"

"Let's try talking to the sheep," Quinn said.

Aisha nodded, and flew back over to the huddle of pink sheep.

"Hello there! What's going on?" Aisha asked a tiny pink lamb, who was wobbling on his skinny legs near the edge of the group.

"The grown-ups have found a mirror. Now all they want to do is stare at themselves," bleated the lamb, rolling his eyes. "We're Sunset Sheep, so we should be busy forming clouds with our wool and sending them up into the sky, ready for when the sun goes down. But since the grown-ups found that mirror, all our cloud work has stopped."

"They're just staring into the mirror?" asked Aisha.

The lamb nodded. "Boring, huh? The worst part is, it makes them *so* unhappy. They only see what's wrong. They can't seem to find anything good about themselves! My sisters and I have decided not to look."

"Good thinking," Aisha said to the little Sunset Lamb. She turned to Mei and Quinn. "It's *got* to be the Magic Mirror, right?" she said.

"Definitely," agreed Mei and Quinn.

Aisha still didn't know how they were going to get the mirror back. "I'm going to just try asking them," decided Aisha.

She hovered above the flock. "Sunset Sheep!" she called. "Please move away from the mirror.

It is dangerous! We are Treasure Dragon Girls, and we have come to take it back to the Forest Vault, where it belongs."

The sheep paid no attention at all. They didn't even look up!

Quinn joined in. "You have to stop looking

into the mirror," she urged. "It just shows you what you're worried about. You don't really look like that."

"That's right!" added Mei. "You are all fluffy and adorable and totally gorgeous. Please go back to work. The sunset won't be the same without your woolly clouds!"

"You're just saying that," bleated one sheep. "We can see how we really look now."

"We can't possibly create sunset clouds at the moment. We can only do that when we feel happy. If we tried, the clouds wouldn't float up. They would be gray and heavy, like rocks," baaed another.

"That mirror is making them so anxious that

they can't move." Quinn sighed. "Now I under-
stand why the Tree Queen said it was dangerous."

"Maybe we just grab it and fly off?" Aisha
said, thinking hard.

"I don't know if that's such a good idea,"
Quinn said.

"I know. But we have to do something!" Aisha
insisted.

She was so frustrated! She drew in a deep
breath and let out a roar. Startled, the sheep
looked up. Aisha zoomed down toward the
mirror. She grasped hold of the mirror's gilt
frame with her strong talons. Yes! But as she
tried to lift it up and away, the Sunset Sheep
started batting their hooves at Aisha.

"Oh no you don't!" they baaed furiously. "The mirror stays with us!"

"It's bad for you! Can't you see that?" called Mei.

"It's not baaaad! We need it!"

Aisha could feel her talons losing their grip on the slippery mirror. "Mei, Quinn! Help!" she called.

Her friends soared over, ready to help. But the Sunset Sheep were stronger than they looked. They tugged on the mirror and it fell from Aisha's grasp. As it landed, it hit a rock jutting out from the snow.

Then, with a terrible sound, the Magic Mirror cracked in two.

5

"Oh no!" Aisha groaned as she landed heavily on the ground.

She couldn't believe it! Treasure Dragons were meant to protect the Magic Forest's precious objects, not break them! What would happen now that the mirror was broken?

"Aisha, it wasn't your fault," said Quinn quickly.

"It could've happened to any of us," agreed Mei.

Aisha nodded but didn't reply. Her friends were being nice, but she felt terrible. And she was worried, too. What were they going to do?

Just then, Aisha felt a nudge. PlushyPup! "You must get the pieces of mirror away from here as quick as you can!" he said.

Even as he spoke, the sky darkened, as if the sun had gone behind the clouds.

"What's going on?" cried Quinn.

Aisha looked up at a swirling mass above them.

"Watch out. Shadow Sprites!" yelled Mei.

The Sunset
Sheep began
bleating very
loudly. From
every direc-
tion, Shadow

Sprites streaked down
toward the group. Confused, the Sunset
Sheep scattered in all directions, baaing at
the top of their lungs. The Shadow Sprites
continued their attack. More and more of
them appeared, darting across the snow
toward the panicking pink sheep, leaving
gray marks in the crisp white snow.

The two halves of the broken mirror were

lying on the snow, unprotected. The gilt frame had broken along with the mirror itself.

"Quick, grab the pieces!" PlushyPup urged.

Aisha tried to move, but she was frozen in place. She wanted to help the poor sheep, and she wanted to grab the mirror pieces. But her whole body felt heavy. It was as though the snow around her paws had just gotten extra heavy.

"I can't move!" Quinn called.

"Me neither!" Mei said. "Maybe we've become Snow Dragons!"

Aisha's brain whirred. They had to warm up— and fast! But how? There was only one way.

"On the count of three, let's roar!" Aisha said.

She *really* hoped this would work. "One, two, three!"

The Dragon Girls all roared. Instantly, the freezing air around them filled with warmth. Their ruby, sapphire, and jade roars swirled in the air like a tumbling ball of magic. Aisha felt the heat wrap around her like a loving hug, thawing her out.

"Good thinking, Aisha," said Mei, flapping her wings and lifting off the ground.

From above them came a strange buzzing noise. As Aisha watched in alarm, the cloud of Shadow Sprites changed into the shape of an arrow. And that arrow was streaking down toward the broken mirror!

"We've got to grab the pieces before they do!" Aisha cried.

The Treasure Dragons launched into the air. Down below, Aisha could see the first piece of mirror. Just as she swooped down to grab it, she was swamped by Shadow Sprites. Everything went dark. Aisha couldn't tell what was up or down. She felt that horrible cold seeping into her wings again. The sprites muttered mean things as they brushed against her.

"You can't possibly win against us! Give up, Treasure Dragon. There's no point in trying," a chorus of sprites hissed.

That made Aisha mad! "I will never give up!" she roared, flapping her wings and rising higher. "And neither will my friends!"

The reaction was quick. The sprites fled from the warmth and power of her roar. But when the air cleared, Aisha saw something terrible down below: The two halves of the mirror had disappeared.

"They're going that way!" shouted Mei, pointing.

Sure enough, there was a tight group of Shadow Sprites, flying away with one half of the Magic Mirror.

"But there are others going *that* way!" called Quinn. She pointed in the opposite direction, to another group of Shadow Sprites moving away swiftly with the other half of the Magic Mirror.

"Who do we follow?" Quinn asked.

"Should we split up?" Mei said.

Aisha hesitated. It really did make sense to split into two groups.

But then PlushyPup whispered in her ear. "Remember what the Tree Queen said?"

Aisha nodded, the queen's words ringing in her head. *The Shadow Sprites will try to divide you.*

"No, we stick together," she said firmly. "Come on!"

Aisha took off after the closest group of Shadow Sprites. "We'll get one half of the mirror back. *Then* we'll go after the other half."

The cold air didn't bother the Shadow Sprites. They streaked ahead with the mirror held aloft among them. It shone like it was made from polished silver.

"Let's just keep going. We'll catch them in the end," Aisha called to her friends.

There was no
way she was
going to fail this
quest. She flapped
her wings as hard
as she could, lov-
ing the feeling of
power it gave her.

The sprites led them farther and farther

away. Before long, Aisha could see the snow-

capped mountains at the edge of the Magic

Forest. The Dragon Girls flew so high that

the air grew even colder and thinner, making

it hard to breathe. But Aisha barely noticed.

With each moment that passed, she and her

friends were gaining on the Shadow Sprites. They were close enough now to see snowflakes falling on the Magic Mirror as the sprites carried it along.

They were high in the mountains now. The snow was so dazzlingly white that it was hard to see. But Aisha kept her eyes trained on the shadowy mass until she was so close she could just about reach out and touch them.

"You've almost got them!" called Mei and Quinn from behind.

But as Aisha stretched out a talon, the Shadow Sprites turned the shard of Magic Mirror to face her.

"Don't look!" yelped PlushyPup.

"Close your eyes, everyone!" Aisha called as she squeezed hers shut.

She kept her eyes closed for only a couple of seconds. But when she opened them again, the Shadow Sprites—and the piece of Magic Mirror—had vanished.

"Where did they go?" Aisha asked, scanning the ground below.

"I don't know," admitted Mei. "It all happened so fast."

"I'm not sure, either," said Quinn. "What should we do?"

PlushyPup spoke up. "My family lives in this

part of the forest. They might know which way the Shadow Sprites went."

"Okay. Let's land here and ask your family," said Aisha.

It sure felt like they could use some help.

PlushyPup and the three Treasure Dragons swooped lower and landed beside a huge, beautiful lake. All around the lake were tall snow-covered trees and towering mountains. Icicles hung from the tree branches, shining like crystals. The frozen surface of the lake sparkled in the light like it was filled with diamonds. The cold air smelled faintly of peppermint.

Even Aisha had to admit that winter could

be beautiful!

"This is the Diamond Lake," PlushyPup said

proudly. "My family lives really close."

"How do we find them?" Aisha asked.

PlushyPup didn't answer. Instead, he tipped

back his head, closed his eyes, and let out a long howl. The howl bounced off the surrounding mountains in an echo. It sounded like there were a hundred howling puppies, not just one!

When PlushyPup stopped, the group stood still, waiting. Nothing happened.

"That's strange," said PlushyPup. "Normally someone appears right away."

Aisha was about to suggest that PlushyPup howl again when Mei gave a sudden shout.

"Hey! Look over there!"

In the center of Diamond Lake was a group of sparkly white bears. They all had silky scarves wrapped elegantly around their necks. And around their impressive waists the bears wore matching tutus. Even stranger, the bears were gliding across the frozen surface of the lake on their hind legs.

Mei squinted. "Are those bears wearing skates?"

"And tutus?" added Aisha.

"Yes, of course," said PlushyPup. "They are the famous Gliding Bears. They put on the most amazing concerts."

Aisha watched as the bears pirouetted and twirled, their scarves streaming out behind them. Sometimes they held out their arms to the sides for balance; sometimes they held them up above their heads or tucked them in tight to twirl even faster. The bears were very

big and strong,
but they still
seemed to float
across the ice.

"Let's go over
and ask them if
they've seen the
Shadow Sprites,"
said Mei.

"It looks like they are rehearsing," said
PlushyPup. "We must wait until they are
finished."

"But we don't have time to wait," Aisha
pointed out. "The Shadow Sprites will be getting farther and farther away."

"Hey, look!" Quinn pointed. "They've stopped skating. What are they doing?"

The bears were standing in a circle, waving their paws around wildly and growling at one another.

"Maybe it's part of the performance?" Mei suggested.

But Aisha just knew something was up. The bears were obviously upset! Then Aisha noticed a shape sticking up out of the ice. The shape had a gilt frame.

"The mirror! We need to get over there," Aisha said, getting ready to fly across.

"You'll have to skate over," warned PlushyPup. "The Gliding Bears won't talk to you otherwise."

"But I can't skate!" said Aisha. "And besides, we don't have any skates."

"We'll go together," said Mei. "On our paws."

"Of course we will," said Quinn.

Aisha was still worried. "Is the ice strong enough to hold us as well as all the bears?"

"Oh yes," said PlushyPup. "The Diamond Lake ice is extremely hard. Only something very, very powerful could break it."

Mei and Quinn linked their wings around Aisha's and together they stepped onto the ice. Aisha felt her paws slipping in all directions. "I don't know if I can do this!" she said in a wobbly voice.

The bears looked very far away right now.

"You can do this, Aisha," said Quinn kindly but firmly.

"Try sliding your paws instead of taking steps," said Mei.

Aisha tried, and it was definitely easier. Soon she began to get the hang of it. But she was very glad that she had her friends there just in case!

As they approached the bears, Aisha could finally hear what they were saying.

"We'll have to cancel tonight's show. We can't possibly perform now *this* is here."

"The show was going to be a disaster any-way! We made so many mistakes during rehearsal. It was the worst we've ever skated."

"The Magic Mirror is definitely messing up their rehearsal," Mei whispered.

"Let's get over there now!" urged Quinn.

In no time at all, the Treasure Dragons were right near the bears.

"No one will come to our shows ever again. We're ruined!" growled one bear.

"I look ridiculous in this tutu," moaned another.

A few bears burst into loud, growly tears.

"We think you look great. And we'd love to see your performance!" Aisha called.

The bears stopped their wailing and turned to stare at the Dragon Girls.

"We've heard you are the best skaters in

the whole forest," added Quinn.

"We used to think so," said one of the bears sadly. "But everything is going wrong at the moment! This

big thing dropped out of the sky and got stuck in our lake. But who cares? We're no good at skating and we look silly in these tutus. We can see that now."

"You don't look silly at all," said Quinn. "You look amazing! You are powerful and elegant. And the way you move is just magic."

But the bears didn't seem to hear. They had begun to cry again as they gazed at their reflections in the half mirror. Clearly, it hadn't lost its power when it had been smashed in two.

One or two bears blew their noses on their pretty scarves. Others used their great furry paws to mop their eyes.

Beyond the bears, Aisha could see the mirror sticking out of the lake. She took care not to look into it.

"I have an idea," she whispered to Mei and Quinn. "Let's get the bears to do their show for us. Then while they are distracted, one of us can grab the piece of mirror."

"Do you think we'll be able to talk them into doing it?" said Quinn.

"We have to," said Aisha firmly. "Because if we don't, I am not sure what else to do!"

Aisha turned to face the bears. She wasn't quite sure what she was going to say to them, but she knew it had to be good. She opened her mouth to speak, but her paws slipped in different directions. She fell—splat—on the ice. As she tried to stand up, she slipped again, landing on her tail. Aisha wasn't much good at

skating as a human girl, but as a dragon she found it virtually impossible! A strange growly noise filled the air.

Aisha looked at the bears. "Are you laughing at me?" she asked, laughing herself as she tried to stand up straight.

"Sorry," said a bear with a glittery silver

scarf and matching tutu. "But you are a really bad skater!"

"I know." Aisha sighed. "How about you show me how it's done? I *really* need some tips."

The bears put their heads together and spoke in quiet, deep voices. Then the silver-scarfed bear looked back at Aisha. "We will do a short routine for you, but only if your dragon friends join in."

"We'd LOVE to!" said Mei.

"Let's go over there," suggested Quinn. "The ice is smoother."

She winked at Aisha as she and Mei led the bears away from the mirror shard.

As the bears began to skate, the wind jangled

the icicles dangling from the trees. They made a tinkling, bell-like sound. Beams of soft light fell in shafts across the icy lake, gleaming like spotlights.

Faster and faster the bears skated, twirling and leaping with strength and grace. Their tutus fluttered. Mei and Quinn tried to follow along, and soon the bears held on to their paws to include them in the routine. Aisha felt a little pang as they all whooshed over the smooth ice in complicated patterns. She wished she were part of the dance!

But I have a job to do, she reminded herself. *We can come back another time, and I'll learn how to skate then.*

Aisha slid carefully over to the mirror shard, which was jutting out of the ice. It was snowing again, and the mirror was half-covered in fresh snow.

"I'll help you dig it out," said PlushyPup. He began digging at the snow furiously with his front paws. Snow sprayed in all directions. Aisha dug, too. But it seemed that no matter how hard they dug, they could not get through the pile of snow. It felt like they weren't getting anywhere!

And then Aisha heard a noise. Looking up, she saw a bright blue puppy with big blue eyes, fluttering in the sky above her.

"PlushyPup?" Aisha called, confused.

But PlushyPup was still next to her! And now that she looked closely, Aisha saw the puppy above her was even smaller than PlushyPup.

"It's TrustyPup, my little sister!" barked PlushyPup in delight. "What are you doing here?"

"I've come to help you, of course," said the tiny puppy, landing in the snow.

Aisha wasn't sure how much help this teensy creature would be. But the moment TrustyPup started digging, snow went flying everywhere.

TrustyPup was small, but she was an excellent digger. With her there, PlushyPup seemed to dig even faster, too.

Soon, the shard of mirror began to budge.

Aisha's heart thumped with excitement. "Keep digging!" she called to the hardworking puppies. "I am going to try and pull the mirror out of the ice."

Being careful not to look into it, Aisha gripped the mirror's frame with her claws. She tugged and tugged ... but the mirror was stuck.

The sky darkened, as if a big storm cloud had formed overhead. But Aisha knew it wasn't really a storm cloud. Looking up, she saw masses of Shadow Sprites swirling above. One sprite pulled itself from the pack and lunged down at her. As it wrapped around her wing, Aisha felt a coldness spread through her.

"Who are you kidding, Dragon Girl?" the Shadow Sprite hissed. "You'll never get the mirror out of the ice and back into one piece."

PlushyPup and TrustyPup barked furiously. They snapped at the sprite while Aisha shook her wing as hard as she could. Finally, the sprite let go and returned to the pack.

But soon, another sprite flew at them. And another, and another! Each time they attacked, PlushyPup and his sister fought them back while Aisha worked on pulling out the piece of mirror. But it just would not move! The worst part was that the sprites' taunts were starting to get to her. *Maybe they're right. I'll probably never get the mirror back into one piece or return it to the vault.*

At the sound of beating wings, Aisha turned to see a wonderful sight: Mei and Quinn were flying toward her!

"C'mon! We'll pull out that mirror together," Mei cried as she and Quinn landed on either side of Aisha.

This drove the hovering Shadow Sprites crazy! They flew at the Dragon Girls and the puppies, slithering around them and trying to catch them.

But now that her friends were beside her, Aisha felt strong and sure. The Treasure Dragon Girls would get this task done!

The three friends gripped the mirror and pulled.

"It's moving!" Quinn yelled excitedly.

She was right. Aisha could feel it shifting. It felt like a wobbly tooth, one that was ready to come out. "Right, on the count of three," said Aisha. "One, two three . . . pull!"

Two things happened at once. The ice creaked as the mirror finally came loose, and a Shadow Sprite darted toward TrustyPup, yanking her up into the air.

"TrustyPup!" howled PlushyPup, flying up to grab her.

But the little pup didn't need her big brother's help. With a fierce growl, TrustyPup ripped at the Shadow Sprite with her sharp little teeth until it let her go.

"Quick! Catch her!" yelled Aisha.

It was too late. TrustyPup had already fallen onto the hard ice below.

The Shadow Sprites twisted and spun around overhead, hissing. They were furious! But so was Aisha.

How dare they hurt PlushyPup's little sister! A huge roar burst out of her, warming the cold air and making it shimmer with gold-flecked blue fire. It was the first time her roar had had gold in it, too. This was a true Treasure Dragon roar!

Mei and Quinn joined in, and the sound of their roar echoed through the snowy landscape, making the icicles jangle and crackle. The Treasure Dragons' roar was so powerful that the Shadow Sprites scattered.

Aisha slipped the Magic Mirror shard into the bag the Tree Queen had given her. It was much too big for the bag. It shouldn't have fit at all! But both the mirror and the bag were magical, so it did.

"Let's get this little pup to safety," Aisha said, gently scooping up TrustyPup with a wing and putting her on her back. She knew the Shadow Sprites wouldn't stay away for long. TrustyPup was being very brave, but the fall had left her with a nasty cut on her front leg.

"I'll show you the way to our den," yapped PlushyPup.

The group rose into the air, following PlushyPup.

"Goodbye, Dragon Girls!" called the Gliding Bears from down below. "Thanks for remind-ing us that we can skate, after all!"

They flew above even more snow-covered trees and frozen lakes. Aisha was flying carefully, as she didn't want to scare little TrustyPup. But then the brave pup called out, "Faster and higher, please!" so Aisha picked up her pace.

In the distance, Aisha could see a strange shape. At first she thought it was an enormous iceberg—but there are no icebergs in the mountains! As they got closer, Aisha saw it had windows and turrets on the top. It was somehow both beautiful *and* scary.

PlushyPup flew up beside her. "That's the Shadow Queen's palace," he explained.

Aisha shivered. No wonder the place had given her the creeps!

"Our den is down here," yapped TrustyPup.

They zoomed down toward a thicket of trees. The Dragon Girls followed close behind. Aisha was careful not to let TrustyPup slip from her back as she descended. Hidden behind the trees was the entrance to a cave.

The Dragon Girls landed nearby. PlushyPup scampered through the space easily, but it was more difficult for Aisha, Mei, and Quinn, who were much bigger. Aisha tucked TrustyPup

under her wing for safety and wiggled through

the entrance. Once she was through, she stood

up and looked around.

They were in the coziest cave Aisha had ever

seen. The floor was covered in thick, shaggy

rugs. A cheerful fire flickered in one corner.

The cave had a comforting smell that reminded Aisha of baking in her grandmother's kitchen.

A magnificent husky bounded over. She was the same deep blue color as PlushyPup but with silver markings around her face instead of gold. On her back was a pair of powerful wings. "What's going on?" she barked loudly.

"Mom!" yapped PlushyPup. "The Shadow Sprites hurt TrustyPup," he explained. "Look, she's been cut!"

Gently, Aisha placed the shivering puppy on the rug near the fire. The mother dog sniffed and licked TrustyPup's injured paw.

Aisha, Mei, and Quinn looked on anxiously.

How terrible it would be if this brave little puppy was badly hurt!

"She will be fine," said the huskies' mom, finally.

The Dragon Girls all sighed in relief.

"I will put some of my special ointment on the cut," continued the mother. "Could you get it for me, please? It's in a bowl over there on the shelves in the corner."

Aisha was pleased to help and hurried over to the shelves. As she was picking up the bowl of ointment, something glimmered in the light. Aisha almost dropped the ointment in surprise. Leaning against the wall of the cave was a broken shard of mirror with a gilt frame. It was identical to the piece in her bag!

Aisha hurried back to the mother dog with the ointment. Her heart was thumping with excitement. "Guys, look!" she said, pointing to the mirror shard.

Quinn gasped. "The missing piece of the Magic Mirror!"

"How did it get in here?" marveled Mei.

"I found that out in the snow just before you got here," replied the mother dog as she lovingly dabbed ointment on TrustyPup's cut. "It smelled like trouble, so I brought it down here for safekeeping."

PlushyPup bounded over to Aisha. "Go on!" he barked. "See if the two halves fit together."

Trembling with excitement, Aisha pulled the

other piece of mir-
ror from her bag.
She padded over to
the piece leaning
against the wall.
As she got closer,
she felt the mir-
ror pulling toward

the other piece, like a magnet that wanted to

touch another.

Being very careful not to look into the mir-

ror, Aisha brought the two sections close to

each other. With a burst of light, the halves of

the mirror clicked together.

"You did it!" cheered Mei and Quinn.

"No, we did it," said Aisha, wrapping a wing around each friend and pulling them close. "Wow, the mirror looks perfect! You can't even tell that it was broken."

"You're right," said Mei. "There's no crack at all. Even the frame has joined up perfectly."

"And look at how clear our reflection is," Aisha added.

"Hang on! We're not supposed to look into the mirror!" Quinn gasped.

Mei frowned. "It is supposed to make us see our faults, and all the things we worry about. I don't see anything like that, do you?"

Aisha shook her head. "All I see is an amazing team of Treasure Dragon Girls."

"Me too," said Quinn.

PlushyPup fluttered over. "Maybe when a team works really well together, the mirror has no power over you," he woofed, wagging his tail superfast.

"That actually makes sense." Aisha smiled at her friends. She was so glad that she was one of the Treasure Dragon Girls!

PlushyPup nudged Aisha with his nose. "It's time to go. You must return the mirror to the vault. I will show you the way back."

Aisha nodded. She knew PlushyPup was right. The Magic Mirror was clearly very powerful. The sooner it was safely back in the vault, the better!

TrustyPup, who was snuggled by her mother's side, looked up brightly. "Can I come, too?" she barked. "I feel totally fine now."

"You are one tough cookie." Aisha smiled. "But you should rest. Thanks so much for your help. We couldn't have done it without you."

Their mother walked over and nuzzled each of the Dragon Girls in turn. "Thank you for protecting the treasures of the Magic Forest!"

"It's our pleasure," said Mei and Quinn happily.

"And it's our job!" added Aisha, her insides bursting with pride.

Outside the cave, the sky was the color of lead. "I think a snowstorm is coming," said Quinn.

"Let's get going before it arrives," said Mei. "I don't want to be flying through a storm."

Neither did Aisha! She had another worry, too. The sprites were going to be hard to spot against that gray sky.

They said one last goodbye to TrustyPup and her mom, who were waving at the den's entrance. Little TrustyPup was barking happily and leaping up and around her mom's legs.

The sky grew darker and heavier as the Treasure Dragons flew back the way they'd come. It wasn't long before snow began to fall again, thick and heavy. Large flakes landed on the Dragon Girls' wings, making them cold and stiff. Aisha felt like her whole body was turning into an ice block! The wind had picked up, and it swirled the snow around them as they flew. It was almost impossible to see where they were going. Even worse, Aisha kept feeling Shadow Sprites brushing against her. She could tell that Mei and Quinn were finding it hard as well, but no one complained.

The snowfall grew so heavy that Aisha didn't even notice when PlushyPup flew up alongside her.

"I can't guide us through this storm," he called above the wind. "We must find another way!"

"What other way is there?" Aisha called back.

"These mountains are full of tunnels," PlushyPup explained. "I've heard one of them leads directly to the vault. If we can find it, then we can get out of this storm."

"Sounds good," Aisha panted. The effort of flying in the terrible weather was wearing her out.

"Sure does," Mei called.

"How do we find it?" Quinn asked.

Aisha felt something tug gently at her neck. She looked down to see the compass, glowing on its chain in the darkness. Of course! She had totally forgotten about it. This was the perfect time to ask it for help.

She lifted the compass with one claw. "Where is the tunnel that leads to the vault?" she asked.

Instantly, the golden hand on the compass began to spin around and around. It whirred so fast that the compass jumped out of Aisha's paw! With the chain straining at Aisha's neck, the compass pointed directly down.

"The tunnel is below us!" Aisha shouted to the others. "Come on!"

Aisha swooped down low, PlushyPup and the other Dragon Girls close behind. Just before Aisha landed, the compass swerved to the side and led them into a dark cave.

"I sure hope that compass knows where it's going," muttered Mei.

Aisha did, too! She knew that it was a very

old treasure. What if it had lost its magical sense of direction?

The cave narrowed into a tunnel and began to lead down into the mountain. Soon it was too narrow to fly and the Dragon Girls had to crawl. The surface of the tunnel was icy and slippery, so they half slid and half crawled along.

"It's strange," Quinn commented, "but I swear it's getter lighter the deeper we go."

"Look up and you'll see why!" barked PlushyPup.

The Treasure Dragons looked up and gasped. The roof of the tunnel was studded with tiny yellow lights, twinkling like stars.

"They're sparkle bugs," explained PlushyPup. "Watch. They'll change color in a moment." Sure enough, the yellow lights soon changed to aqua. Next they turned purple.

"Hey!" said Mei. "Let's try sliding along on our stomachs! I bet we'll go superfast that way."

"Awesome idea," said Aisha. She dropped to her stomach, tucked her wings into her side, and pushed off with her claws.

Whoosh! She shot along the slippery tunnel at top speed! She could hear Mei and Quinn whooping with laughter as they slid along behind her. Even PlushyPup tried sliding, though he was small enough to fly.

The tunnel became steeper and the Dragon Girls whooshed faster and faster. They were hurtling deep into the belly of the mountain. Aisha just hoped the compass was leading them to the right place.

Finally, the tunnel leveled off and the Dragon Girls slowed down. They came to a stop in front of a solid wall of rock.

"Please tell me it's not a dead end." Mei groaned.

Aisha frowned. Were they lost? From inside the bag, Aisha felt the mirror quiver. "I think the mirror knows we're close," she said.

PlushyPup came skidding to a stop next to the Dragon Girls. He stood up and sniffed at the wall. "We're definitely close. I can smell treasure on the other side of this rock!"

That was good to know. The only question now was how to get through.

First Aisha, Mei, and Quinn tried pushing at the rock with all their might. But even with all their Dragon Girls strength at work, the rock didn't budge. Aisha felt frustration building. It was so annoying to get so close and then not be able to finish the quest.

"If only this rock would disappear!" she roared.

There was the sound of crumbling rock.

"That made something happen," Mei cried. "Roar again!"

Aisha did, and this time they saw pebbles and dust slide off the rock wall. She squinted at the gap that had opened up in the wall. There was something embedded deep in the rock.

"It's a door handle," Quinn said in wonder.

A glimmer of light beamed through the key-hole beneath the handle.

"C'mon, Treasure Dragons," said Aisha. "There's treasure to protect, and that's what we do best. Let's roar our way in, on my count. One, two, three!"

The Treasure Dragon Girls roared their loudest roar. Pebbles and dirt tumbled down, creating a thick plume of dust in the tunnel. Once it cleared, Aisha and her friends saw something wonderful: an ancient wooden door.

"I hope it's not locked," Aisha joked.

As she reached out a paw to try the door, it swung open.

Golden light flooded in. Aisha squinted at the sudden brightness, her heart thumping. Before them was a huge cave filled with glimmering treasure. The vault!

"We did it!" she cried.

PlushyPup fluttered at her side. "Better get in there quickly," he woofed warningly. "I can hear Shadow Sprites coming."

Aisha paused to listen. From down in the tunnel came a hissing, chattering sound. Quickly, the Dragon Girls

and PlushyPup stepped through the doorway and into the magnificent vault. The door clicked closed behind them.

There were so many beautiful things! Gold coins and twinkling gemstones covered the floor. Intricate diamond necklaces dangled from the tree roots that pushed through the ceiling. Gleaming plates and goblets etched with lacy designs were stacked in every corner. It was like a supercharged antique store. Aisha could have spent all day admiring the gorgeous things.

Toward the back of the huge room were three columns. On each column was a label. Aisha and her friends had already returned the Forest Book to its column. Being very careful not to disturb the treasure lying everywhere, she padded over to the one labeled *Magic Mirror*.

She felt the mirror move again in the bag. Aisha patted it. "Don't worry, we're returning you to where you belong."

She opened the bag
and pulled out the mir-
ror, carefully placing it
on the stand atop the
column. It clicked into
place and looked so...
right.

"Is it just me, or does the mirror look extra

shiny?" commented Quinn.

Aisha nodded. "It definitely does."

"Hey, let's see what the Forest Book has to

say about all this," Mei said.

Mei opened up the heavy book they had res-

cued on their last quest. "*The Treasure Dragon*

Girls returned the Magic Mirror to its rightful place," she read out loud. "*The mirror gleamed brighter than ever, happy to be safely back in the vault. Then PlushyPup fluttered over to Aisha's side . . .*"

Mei stopped reading and looked up. PlushyPup was indeed right there, next to Aisha!

"It's time to see the Tree Queen. Let's go out the front way this time," he suggested, wagging his blue tail superfast.

As Mei closed the Forest Book and carefully put it back, the Treasure Dragons took one last look at the mirror. As they watched, the beautiful golden vines carved into the frame started turning green! Then red, yellow, purple, and blue flowers appeared. It felt like a sign that spring was finally on its way.

There was now only one empty column. The label on it read *Heartstring Violin*.

"I guess returning the Heartstring Violin will be our next mission, right?" said Aisha.

Quinn looked dreamy. "I can't wait," she whispered.

Aisha gazed at all the glorious treasure before flying to the front entrance of the vault with her friends.

The stone slid open as they approached.

"Treasure Dragons!" boomed a voice as they walked through. "I thought I heard you in there."

Aisha turned to see Stone Face. "Hi, Stoney! The Magic Mirror is back, safe and sound. Hopefully the weather will go back to normal soon."

"Wonderful news!" Stone Face beamed. "I just hate the cold. Icicles were starting to form on my nose. The soldier ants kept laughing at me."

"Well, your icicles are all gone now!" Aisha told him with a smile. "We have to go, but we'll be back again soon!"

Together, the three friends soared into the air. High above the Magic Forest, Aisha could see the snow was melting and spring was returning. Bright flowers were already sprouting and the sun sparkled on new green leaves.

A family of minifoxes scampered around, snapping at one another's aqua-spotted tails. It was like the forest was waking up after a long sleep. A warm breeze brushed against Aisha's wings as she and the others zoomed toward the Tree Queen's glade.

"There's the glade!" PlushyPup barked. "I'll head home now to check on TrustyPup."

"Thanks for your help, PlushyPup," said Aisha. "And say hi to your sister!"

"I will!" woofed the little blue puppy as he veered off toward his home, far away in the mountains.

Aisha, Mei, and Quinn glided down to land on the grass next to the glade. They were expert flyers now! Aisha breathed in deeply as she and her friends stepped through the glade's force field. The air always smelled so delicious inside the glade!

They padded on the velvet-soft grass to the Tree Queen, who was already transforming into her queenly form.

"Well done, Treasure Dragon Girls!" said the Tree Queen, smiling her wise smile at them. "I am so happy with how well you did. Now it's time for you to return to your homes."

The Tree Queen reached out a long arm and Aisha handed back the bag and the compass. Then the Tree Queen returned the three magical friendship bracelets to each Dragon Girl. In

front of Mei landed the ruby one, and in front

of Quinn the jade one. Aisha reached down to

pick up her sapphire-blue bracelet. As she did

so, she felt a little sad that the quest had ended

already.

In her wisdom, the Tree Queen seemed to

know how Aisha was feeling. "Don't forget, there

is still one more piece of treasure that needs to be returned to the vault: the Heartstring Violin. Be ready, Dragon Girls! I will be calling you back very soon."

Then, with a rustle of her leaves and a swish of her moss-green gown, she turned back into a tree.

The Treasure Dragons gave one another big wing hugs.

"See you soon!" said Aisha.

She felt so lucky to be friends with Mei and Quinn in the normal world. That made it easier to return home. She looked down at the blue bead in her bracelet. It was glowing, just like it had when she'd first entered the Magic Forest.

As she watched, a beam of blue light shot from it, like a projec-tor. In the glow Aisha could see the antique shop! Aisha took one  last look around at the forest.

"Goodbye for now, Magic Forest," she whis-pered. "I'll be back before you know it."

She closed her eyes and stepped into the light.

"Aisha?" asked a voice. "Ah! There you are."

Aisha opened her eyes to see her

grandmother, walking over to her from the back of the shop. "I am so sorry, my dear. I lost track of time. You must have been so bored, waiting for me while I chatted to the owner."

Aisha gave her grandmother a hug. "I wasn't bored at all," she said. "Actually, the time just flew!"

Turn the page for a special sneak peek of Quinn's adventure!

Quinn hummed to herself as she put her shiny golden trumpet back into its velvet-lined case. Around her, the other band kids chatted loudly as they packed up after practice. Everyone was excited. The big concert was tomorrow night!

Quinn was extra pleased because she had a

new tune in her head. Quinn loved writing her own songs. She looked around. She was too shy to play her own music in front of anyone else. But no one was paying attention. Maybe she could try it now?

Quickly, she pulled her trumpet back out of its case. She loved the smooth metal in her hands. It sometimes felt like her trumpet was a part of her. The loud part! Quinn began to play. The tune in her head flowed through the trumpet and out into the air. She repeated it, building on the melody as she went along. Quinn felt warm inside. It sounded even better than she'd hoped.

"That's beautiful, Quinn! What is it?"

Quinn spun around. Her band leader, Ms. Tran, smiled at her.

"It's not a real s-s-song," stammered Quinn. "I just made it up."

"Oh, it's definitely real," Ms. Tran said. "And it's great. Quinn, I'd like you to play it tomorrow, to kick off our concert. Would you do that for me?"

Quinn's hands went all sweaty. She loved playing in the school band. The way the different instruments all worked together felt like magic. They created something bigger and better than any of the musicians could create on their own. But playing a solo in front of everybody? She really didn't think she could do it.

But Ms. Tran looked so excited, it was hard to say no!

"Maybe," she said, fiddling with the jade-green bead in her friendship bracelet. She had made it with her jewelry-class friends, Mei and Aisha. They were both very brave. They wouldn't be scared about playing a solo.

Ms. Tran looked at her kindly. "You don't have to, Quinn. But it would be lovely to let others hear your music. Think about it and let me know tomorrow?"

"Okay." Quinn nodded as Ms. Tran strolled off, whistling Quinn's new song.

Quinn was about to return her trumpet to its case when she heard singing. It was familiar, but very faint. Where was it coming from? She glanced around the room, which was now empty apart from Ms. Tran, who was stacking music stands.

Outside the window, Quinn saw the forest trees swaying. They seemed to be calling her. Quinn's heart began to beat faster. She was pretty sure she knew what was happening. Recently, she, Mei, and Aisha had discovered that they shared more than a love of making jewelry. They were also Treasure Dragon Girls! It was their job it was to protect the treasure in the Magic Forest. When they were needed, the ruler of the Forest—the Tree Queen—called for them.

Quinn had a feeling this was happening right now! The words of the song were clearer now.

Magic Forest, Magic Forest, come explore …

Excitement swirled inside Quinn. She was definitely being called to the Forest! She glanced down at her friendship bracelet. The jade bead at its center glowed bright green. As she watched, a warm, green light beamed out. The light whooshed around her and then shot into the mouthpiece of her trumpet.

Instantly, the trumpet turned an enchanting shade of green. Then the light beam flowed from the trumpet's bell, wider and brighter than before. The words of the song filled Quinn's ears.

Magic Forest, Magic Forest, come explore...

Quinn glanced over at Ms. Tran. Even though the music was getting louder, her teacher didn't seem to hear it. She was now busy arranging chairs.

Quinn gave her trumpet an affectionate pat. "I'll be back soon," she whispered. "But right now, the Magic Forest needs me."

Quinn looked at the beam of light. She

could see trees inside it now! But these were not the bare, wintry trees like those outside the rehearsal room. These trees had the fresh, green look of spring. Quinn closed her eyes and breathed deeply as a warm breeze wafted past, heavy with the scent of mangoes, coconuts, and vanilla.

When she opened her eyes again, the beam of light was big enough to step into. The song filled her ears and she opened her mouth and sang loud and true.

Magic Forest, Magic Forest, come explore.
Magic Forest, Magic Forest, hear my roar!

Taking a deep breath, Quinn stepped into the beam of light. The rehearsal room faded away. The green glow wrapped around Quinn, lifting her up into the air.

She was off on an adventure!

ABOUT THE AUTHORS

Maddy Mara is the pen name of Australian creative duo Hilary Rogers and Meredith Badger. Hilary and Meredith have been collaborating on books for children for nearly two decades.

Hilary is an author and former publishing director, who has created several series that have sold into the millions. Meredith is the author of countless books for kids and young adults, and also teaches English as a foreign language to children.

The Dragon Girls is their first time co-writing under the name Maddy Mara, the melding of their respective daughters' names.

Oh my glaciers, Diary!

Princess Lina is the *coolest* girl in school!

THE GLITTER DRAGONS

DRAGON GIRLS

We are Dragon Girls, hear us ROAR!

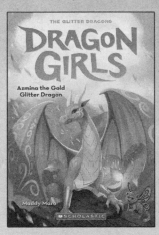

Read all three clawsome Glitter Dragon adventures!

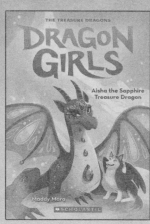